LITTLE BLACK PEARL

PEARL

THE SLAVE PRINCESS

J & J Morris

ISBN 978-1-905553-51-8

Published by Dolman Scott Ltd

www.dolmanscott.com

With Thanks to:
Steve, Sophie, Anne, Gemma and Wendi

Contents

Chapter One

Little Black Pearl

Long ago in a far off land, lived a beautiful little girl: she had black curly hair and big brown eyes, she was seven years old and tall and slender for her age. She wore a loose floral wrap and her brown body shimmered in the sultry sunshine as she played bare foot amongst the mud and straw huts of the village where she lived with her father and mother, the King and Queen.

In this tropical paradise, life was idyllic and could be no better for the King, Queen and little Princess Bonnie, whom they affectionately called their 'Little Black Pearl'. Her father had found a black pearl on a fishing trip at sea many years before when he was a young warrior. He had strung it with beautiful white pearls he had acquired whilst trading, together with the gold engraved emblem of their tribe.

On Bonnie's fifth birthday her father gave her the necklace and she wore it always.

The King and Queen loved their daughter dearly and they ruled their people with great kindness.

One day the Princess and her best friend Bobo, a young boy from her village who was nine years old, decided to go exploring beyond the trees that surrounded their home. They wandered off into the thick forest that encircled the plain where they lived. The dense foliage with its thick fronds, exotic flowers, and tall trees began to hem them in but they picked their way through and happily listened to, and mimicked the sounds of the birds' songs. They made up bird talk and began chanting to each other, laughing and playing and darting in and out of the lush green plants and trees. They were getting nearer to the sparkling waterfall! Bonnie had been told never to venture this far off and she must never go to the waterfall alone. 'But I am not alone.' She thought.

The children stopped for a moment to listen as the roaring sound of the rushing river pouring over the rocky falls, replaced the sounds of the chattering monkeys and twittering birds. They looked at each other and giggled excitedly. Holding hands they ran toward the rocky edge of the plateau where they stood and gasped, watching as the white foamy water cascaded into the hollow below. It fell like beautiful rainbow coloured jewels crashing with a tremendous roar and changing colours as it did, sending up masses of cloudy bubbles like thousands of white pearls dancing on the rocks. They stood captivated by this awesome sight and jumped up and down with pleasure as the fine spray that was caught on the gentle breeze tickled their faces.

Their adventure was over. They had done what they had set out to do. It was now time to return home.

After all their excitement they looked around to realise they were a little unsure which way to head back; they seemed to recognise some of the big trees and headed through them.

'My mother and father will be worried.' Bonnie thought, but she imagined that she and Bobo had not been away for too long.

As the sound of the rushing waterfall faded into the distance the children once again began to sing the birds songs and they joined in with the chattering of the monkeys.

Suddenly, Bobo and Bonnie both halted, as they heard, way off in front of them, what they thought was the sound of the 'danger shell'. They had been warned about such a sound which was blown on a large shell by one of the warriors of the tribe to warn of imminent danger. They could also hear faintly the sounds of the drums but they could not understand them as neither of them was able to read the drums very well. They moved forward swiftly and stealthily through the thick undergrowth but stopped as they heard shouting and desperate cries not far ahead. They came to a clearing cautiously and a dreadful sight was before them. They sank back into the thick undergrowth and hid themselves under the enormous leaves of the tropical plants. They held their hands over their ears and closed their eyes tightly as they sobbed. They knew something terrible was happening to the people of their village; they could hear loud crackling noises and they could smell smoke.

After what seemed to be an age, they peeped out from their hiding place. Some of the huts were on fire and some were smouldering with wisps of white and grey smoke wafting into the air. There was no sound now; even the birds had stopped singing.

Bonnie could see the hut where she lived and she was thankful it had not been burned, but there was no sign of life.

The two children ran from place to place looking and trying to understand what had happened. Their attention was drawn to a noise from the bushes; they stopped in their tracks and clung to each other. Their hearts beat loud as they held their breath, not knowing what was to befall them. Then, came a sigh of relief as children emerged bleeding and crying. The children bowed before their Princess.

She stepped toward them and spoke softly. "What has happened?"

She cradled the youngest girl who sobbed uncontrollably and she wiped away her tears.

"It was the fearful tribe, the one we have all been warned of," answered an older boy, "the ones with hoops in their ears and long thick strands of hair"

"They came with some white men" interrupted another child, "who had fire sticks and the fearful tribe had their spears and knives and ropes. Their Chief was with them."

The older boy who had spoken before continued, "They captured our parents and our brothers and sisters and tied them with rope and took them away." He lowered his head. "They took the King and Queen too."

From beneath her tears the little girl that Bonnie cradled spoke, "They chased us but we ran and hid." She cried more. "I want my mother."

Bobo and Bonnie looked at each other.

"Why have they done this?" Bobo questioned.

"That fearful Chief does not like our peaceful tribe, he has said he will make us leave this land," answered the older boy. "I have heard our tribesmen talk of it. He will sell his prisoners to the white man and they will take them to a far off land where they will be made slaves. The fearful Chief will get many good things in exchange."

Bonnie had also heard talk of this but she had not really understood. She began to recall when the King and Queen had told her of white men and how some were very bad. She was told of the slave boats that carried the black man to a land where he was made to work hard and treated like an animal, caged and chained at night and fed very little. It was then they had told her of many dangers and hoped that she would always listen to their counsel as they loved her very much and did not want harm of any kind to come to her.

Bonnie looked at the young girl she was cradling. "I want my mother too," she said, "and I'm going to find her!" She stood up and looked at the village huts smoldering. She turned to Bobo and the other children with a determined look on her face. "We must do something."

Bonnie did not want her mother and father to be slaves or to be treated like animals. She decided she was going to follow their trail. Bobo agreed.

Chapter Two

To The Rescue

Bonnie took the children into her family's hut where there was still plenty of food. She told them that soon they would return bringing back other members of the tribe. "You must stay together," she said, "look after each other."

Bobo collected what he could for their journey, he found a spear and he had his own knife which his father had helped him make only a short time ago, he thought that these would be very useful.

They took very little food from the hut as they would gather wild fruit and berries on their journey. With nothing to carry they could move swiftly.

They were ready to leave but it was getting dark and the moon was not in the sky this night. They bedded down with the other children.

At first light they were up and ready. They all hugged and Bonnie and Bobo left the village, waving to the children from the forest edge. Following the trail of broken twigs, flower stems and damaged leaves they started on their journey. On occasion they would find a piece of ripped clothing that had got caught on a jagged branch.

Neither Bobo nor Bonnie had ventured this far into the dense forest before and the unfamiliar animal noises, the chattering and snorting, roars and squawks made them uneasy; this was frightening and nothing like the adventure they had had the previous day on their trek to the waterfall. Then, they had felt safe, now they didn't. With every step they felt in danger. Bobo held his spear ready to use and he tried hard to reassure Bonnie as the trail was becoming more difficult to follow.

Every so often bright sunlight filtered through the spaces among the tall, dense trees. This made them feel good and helped give them hope that they would soon find their families and the rest of their tribe.

They were able to find plenty of fruit and berries to eat and as they knew which succulent plants to get juice from, they were not thirsty.

They journeyed for several days and often Bonnie would cry. Bobo would comfort her. He wanted to cry too, but he was now a young warrior and he fought back the tears and spoke words of hope to her. "We will find our families, I am sure of it, we have come so far, it won't be too long now."

The nights seemed long and they slept uneasily, hidden under the dense foliage that they covered themselves with. They huddled together for comfort and reassurance.

They had now been travelling for many long days and nights. They had grown used to the unfamiliar sounds of the forest, but today they heard new sounds. In the distance there was a shushing and a rushing and the cries of gulls. There were other things too, that made them aware and more alert. The forest was thinning out. Fewer trees, more sky. The earth beneath them was loose and sandy. The smell of salt was in the air. They could hear the sea pounding against the rocks. They knew they were approaching their destination. *The coast.*

Bobo reached for Bonnie's hand and stealthily they made their way toward the new noises and smells. Voices in languages they did not understand fell on their ears. They quickly crouched behind some rocks and peered carefully out to see much to-ing and fro-ing from rough looking men.

There was a make shift hut set up on the edge of the trees further up the beach and peering out was the fearful Chief, with two of his tribesmen on guard. Many other men and women from the fearful tribe were dancing and chanting round a crackling fire, their long black hair bouncing, their hooped earrings jangling and the beads about their necks clicking .

Bobo pointed to a place just beyond the fearful Chief's hut. "See, there are the prisoners."

Bonnie gripped his hand tightly.

The children could see white men making their way out onto the long stretch of golden sands. The sea was rolling in with glistening surf dancing and smashing onto the rocks, they could make out on the horizon a big ship anchored way off shore, with one small sail still billowing in the gusty sea breeze. The red sunset lit the sky, dusk was fast approaching, it would soon be dark enough for the children to begin helping their people escape. The sailors were now rowing back to the ship for the night.

The fires burned down and the tribe's people were stretched out on the beach sleeping.

The children cautiously edged out, like darting shadows they made their way along the tree line. Bobo held Bonnie's hand tightly. They could see the two guards outside the fearful Chief's hut were now sitting down dozing. They made loud snorting sounds as their heads drooped, which caused them to wake and shake, but they were soon asleep again.

Tied to trees, close to the hut they saw silhouettes which they now recognised as people from their own village. Bobo was sure he could see his family and he held his breath with anticipation as he studied them a little longer. Yes! It was *his* family, his mother, father and his two brothers. Bonnie looked about for her mother and father. She could not see them and tears welled in her eyes, yet she forced a smile, through her tears, at Bobo because he had found his family.

The two guards were now most definitely asleep, so Bobo pulled Bonnie by the hand and they tip-toed silently for the back of the hut. The prisoners were not asleep when the children came into view and some of them gasped at the sight of them. Bobo put his finger to his lips in a gesture of silence and he proceeded to cut at the ropes with his knife. One by one they quietly made their way into the trees. He had freed his family and most of the prisoners when he heard one of the guards stirring. He cut the last of the men free as the guard leapt at him and Bonnie. The guard shouted and men came running. Bobo, startled and alarmed reached for Bonnie's hand, and they began to run into the trees as fast as their feet would take them. One of the guards grabbed Bonnie's arm and the three fell, Bobo lost his grip of Bonnie's hand.

"Go on," Bonnie screamed at him, "Go on."

It was a hard thing for him to do, but by now the whole camp was up and there was commotion all round as evil guards ran in pursuit of the freed prisoners.

"I will find you," he shouted as he ran onwards. "I *will* find you."

He was gone and Bonnie had to face her fate alone.

Chapter Three

Sign of Royalty

The rescued prisoners, along with Bobo's family, had scattered in all directions into the dense jungle and their pursuers knew that it would be hopeless trying to track them in the dark. They still had many other captives and the ship, even when crammed, would only hold so many prisoners.

Princess Bonnie was taken to the fearful fat Chief, who was still sitting, and he knew at once she was a special captive because of the white pearls, the gold engraved emblem and the single black pearl she wore around her neck.

He pulled the pearls off her and concealed them under his robe.

"I shall make an example of you," he snarled, "you are the child of a King, but those who are here will see you mean nothing." He beckoned to a guard. "Prepare her for sacrifice!"

A guard roughly grabbed her and she pulled back, crying.

"Where are my mother and father?" She screamed at the fearful Chief.

"Gone!" He said and he smirked, "and soon, you will be gone too."

It was not yet fully light and the tide would soon be on the turn. A large rowing boat, with six crew members, was coming ashore. A burley man, dressed in blue ragged trousers, a striped top, and wearing a faded bandana over his plaited brown hair, came to the Chief's hut. He strained his eyes in the gloom.

"Where are the prisoners?" he asked in a rough tone.

"We have them." The Chief looked toward a curve in the bay by a cluster of jagged rocks, "a few escaped" he added, trying to lessen the fact that many of the best and strongest prisoners were among those 'few'.

"How did that happen? What were you all doing? You know we pay well for good working slaves. Where were the guards?"

The sailor did not mince his words. He had no respect for this man, this '*Chief*' who betrayed his own kind.

The Captain of the ship had now joined his men on the beach. He looked about him and heard the boson asking about a child prisoner: "That girl over there," he pointed, "she looks like she would be useful, a bit small, but some of the small ones work well."

"She is the daughter of my enemy. She is a Princess. I am going to make an example of her. She is being prepared for sacrifice. She helped the prisoners to escape," the fearful Chief said, screwing his face into a menacing sneer.

"Princess, aha!" the Captain remarked smugly, "you'll be losing out if you kill *her*. If she is a Princess she will be worth more than the other females. If I can find the right person to buy her we could both make a little more. Why kill her? You have already lost some of the prisoners. You'd be throwing riches away."

The Chief liked the things that the white man brought him. "You are right." He said. "Take her; she is of no use to me. Let her suffer in your stinking ship. Make her work hard." He paused a moment. "You should pay me more for her. *She is a Princess!*"

"How can I be sure she is a Princess? She looks no different from the others, only smaller." The Captain did not want to pay the Chief any more than he had already agreed.

The Chief reached under his robe and brought out Bonnie's pearl necklace. "She was wearing these around her neck. The emblem is the sign of royalty."

The Captain's eyes widened. He snatched the pearls from the fat evil Chief. "These should belong to me as I am taking the girl." He stuffed them into his trousers pocket.

The Chief began to object, but did not continue, as the look from the Captain made him fear for his life. Captain Brunt turned his back on the Chief and began to finger the pearls in his pocket. He knew he was going to get a tidy sum of money for them. He didn't care about the girl.

"I'll make sure she goes to someone who will make her work." he snarled without looking back.

As for paying the Chief more, an extra bottle of rum would make him happy. What did he know about the worth of things?

By now the sun was high and the poor brave Princess was herded like an animal with the other women and girl prisoners into one of the rowboats that had come ashore. Bonnie knew many of the captives, but some were from other tribes. She asked about her mother and father, but no one could help her.

"We know they were captured with us," said one, "but they were taken off somewhere a few days ago. We don't know where."

Princess Bonnie, who had tried to be so brave, began to cry. She became weak with her sobbing and a woman she sat next to put her arms around her and tried to comfort her. One of the sailors prodded the woman and told her to 'shut that kid up'. The woman did not understand the words but his tone was clear. Bonnie forced herself to stop crying and thought of Bobo. She thought of the last words he had said to her; 'I will find you'. She knew he would, she just had to be strong and wait, he would not let her down.

The rowboats reached the ship, which sat low in the water and the prisoners were made to clamber aboard, climbing up the nets that were draped over the sides. They were terrified. There were many sailors on the ship and they were rough and carried knives and guns. Their coarse dirty white skin was burned brown by the sun and most of them had long beards and matted hair.

Captain Brunt bellowed out orders. "Weigh anchor, weigh anchor. Set the main sails. Look lively."

The sailors followed orders and as they did so, they sang a song of the sea.

"Heave ho, heave ho, up with the sails and let the wind blow.
Dance on the waves and off we go.
We'll be home pretty soon if the wind stays fair.
Come on me hearties, no time to spare."

The roughneck crew pulled hard on the ropes and the white billowing sails unfurled, slipping up the masts. One sailor had climbed the rigging to the crows nest, the top most part of the ship, and as the ship got well out to sea he rolled down the flag; the skull and crossbones. This was a pirate slave ship. The trade in human cargo had mostly been stopped, but what did a man like Captain Brunt care about people. He only cared for money and wealth and he didn't care how he got it!

Chapter Four

The Journey Begins

Princess Bonnie and the other girls and women had been pushed down into one hold and the men and boys into another. Although she was sure that Bobo had escaped, a part of her hoped he was in the other hold, perhaps he had sneaked in. He may be attempting to rescue her. The sound of the covers being drawn over the holds and fastened broke her thoughts as the lovely sunshine was now blocked out. It took a few moments for her eyes to adjust to the dimness; every now and again a little sunlight filtered through a thin crack in the cover. It was very hot and damp in their prison and there was no comfort, no seats to sit on, no dried grass beds to lie on, just a few racks and the hard wood boarded floor with shavings scattered about it. There was very little room in this dark *dungeon* but the women tried to make the most of it, helping and looking after one another as best they could.

It was so hot and airless; sleeping was not going to be easy.

They heard lots of clattering above and the pirates sang as they worked. There were loud shouts too, and the sound of feet running to and fro. Bonnie became overwhelmed. She suddenly realised she had never been this far from her home before. She wondered if she would ever see the King and Queen again. She cried quietly and in turn the other girls cried too, but at least most of them were with their mothers. She had no one. A woman spoke comforting words to her. Bonnie rested her head on the woman's lap, her eyes closed and she probably would have fallen to sleep but the ship gave an almighty lunge upwards as it caught the rising waves. It was going to be a long, rough journey.

The wind whistled through the sails and the ship, now far from land, creaked and groaned as it rose up and down on the rough sea. The prisoners wondered where they would end up and what would become of them.

There was no real day or night for the prisoners anymore. It was only when food and water was lowered to them that they caught a glimpse of daylight. Most evenings a few of them at a time had to get out of the hold for a little exercise. When they were on deck they were made to jump up and down, and bend and stretch. It was a wonderful feeling. They breathed in as much fresh air as they could whilst outside, but it was only for a few minutes, then they were back into the hold, into the darkness and the stifling heat and stench.

There was, on this ship, in amongst these dreadful pirates, some kinder, even thoughtful sailors, who on occasion, when it was safe from the prying eyes of Captain Brunt, rolled back the cover a little way so that the prisoners could see the sun and breath in some air, and if it happened to be stormy or raining when this occurred it was even better, as raindrops would fall into the hold and Bonnie and the others would hold their faces upwards so that it cooled them.

Although they were fed every evening, it was never enough to fill them, and it was the same with the water; they were always thirsty, and it was impossible to keep any water to wash with. They were all extremely weak. Their sense of time was no more, they lost count of the days that they were on the ship, one day just rolled into the next and some of them became quite ill from the trials of the journey. Then at last there seemed to be more activity than usual above and the hold was opened fully. Bright sunshine streamed in, and they held their hands over their eyes for a few moments. They were unsure of what was to happen next as the pirates began shouting and beckoning for them to climb the rope ladder up to the deck. Some of them, including Bonnie, were now very weak, and they had to be helped up. Once on deck they breathed in the fresh air and listened as the seagulls squawked above them.

"Well my fine ladies, here it is," a pirate pointed to the land ahead, "this special land will be your new home."

They looked at each other not understanding what he had said, but they saw, in the direction of his gesture, the rolling waves breaking onto the rocks, sending up showers of white foam. They also saw the sandy beach beyond, stretching out onto green tufts and rocky slopes. There were no trees on this beach.

As they stood there on deck they all felt very dirty. Their once clean bright clothes were now very worn and ragged, but they were thankful to be out of the stinking hold that had imprisoned them for so long.

The crew rushed about the ship lowering sails and winding ropes, some stood on guard as the women and girls were ordered to climb down the netting attached to the side of the ship, into the rowing boats. It was difficult as they were all so weak, but they were now heading for dry land.

As the rowboats came to shallow water the prisoners were forced into the sea where they washed themselves. They sighed with the pleasure they felt. Bonnie couldn't remember the last time she felt this good; she was up to her waist in the cool blue green water washing herself and the clothes she was wearing. The rolling waves washed over her and the sand spread and tickled under her feet. She looked about her and thought that she may be able to escape by swimming: she was a good swimmer, she had learned in the cool river that had run through her village, but she knew that she was too weak to try, and besides, where would she go? This land was strange; she knew no-one and would not know or understand the language. Pirates with guns and knives stood on the shoreline, and some sat in the rowing boats watching the prisoners as they washed… there was no escape.

After a while the prisoners were herded to the water's edge where the hot golden sand clung to their feet, and the burning sun dried their clothes. The men, who were in chains, had now joined them on the beach. They too, had washed in the sea, and they were refreshed, and their brown skin glistened in the sunshine.

On the shore, other than the pirates, there were tidily dressed men, wearing fancy clothes and tall hats. Several horse drawn carriages and carts were lined up on the coastal road above. The men prisoners were being studied by these newcomers, and were made to open their mouths so that these men could look inside.

One by one the men were unchained, but still their hands remained tied, and they were taken to one or another carriage or cart. Soon all the men were gone.

'But where to?' Bonnie thought to herself.

It was now the turn of the women and girls, they were lined up and, just like the men, their bodies and the insides of their mouths were checked. One by one the women and girls were being taken away. Bonnie was scared and she hid herself as best she could behind one of the women. A rather large man came along and began to prod the women with a cane he was carrying. "How much do you want for this bunch?" he asked Captain Brunt, "I'll buy them *all* off you for the right price".

Bonnie did not want to be prodded, so she continued to hide behind the ragged clothing of the largest woman in front of her. She hoped he would not poke her with his cane and hoped he would be gone when she finally untwisted herself from the woman's clothing. He hadn't, and her heart was racing as the large man handed over a small purse of money for the last of the women.

"Come on my fine ladies, this is a glorious place to be," he chortled, "you will like this new land."

As he turned to lead the women away he noticed Bonnie curled up on the sand. Captain Brunt had stopped her from leaving with the others.

"What about her?" the large man asked.

"You can have her too," Captain Brunt answered, "But she will cost you a pretty penny. She is a Princess!"

"How much?" the large man enquired

"How much will you give me?" Captain Brunt asked.

"This much!" Came the reply as he held out his hand.

Captain Brunt looked at the coins. "Not enough!"

The large man turned and began to walk away with his purchases.

"She is the daughter of a King and worth much more than that…!" Captain Brunt shouted after him, trying to barter, but to no avail as the large man continued to walk away.

On the beach, there was in the distance, a tall slim man wearing a dark blue suit with gold braided sleeves and gold buttons. He knew what was going on, and he felt sickened to think that there could possibly be a trade in human beings. Slavery had been stamped out where he came from, but here he was on his own and could do nothing to stop this slaver. He walked slowly over to where this trading had taken place and looked with disgust at Captain Brunt.

"You're too late sir." Captain Brunt said apologetically. "There'll be more coming along in a few weeks though."

The tall slim man looked at Bonnie cowering there in front of the Captain. She was now the only prisoner left. She looked up at the man and he smiled at her. He held out his hand toward her as he bent down and spoke softly.

"I have a daughter about your age." he said.

Bonnie did not understand his words but she could tell he was a kind man and she smiled back at him.

'She is a beautiful child,' he thought, 'almost regal'.

"How much do you want for this child?" he asked Captain Brunt

A huge grin appeared on the Captain's face, "Well!" he replied, "This child is special, and affords a special price. The tribal Chief I bought her from told me she is a Princess and it is his wish she be sold for a good price."

"How much do you want for her?" The man asked again.

Captain Brunt told the man she would cost 'a great deal'.

The man pulled coins from his pocket. "Here, I'll give you these." He flipped the coins into the air and the Captain snatched at them eagerly.

He looked at the coins. "I've been robbed!" He snarled. "But she ain't any use to me."

The man took hold of Bonnie's hand and pulled her gently to her feet.

Bonnie was not at all uncomfortable going with this man. It was an unusual feeling that she had. Here she was, being led away by a stranger in an unfamiliar land, but she felt relief instead of fear, and was so glad to be getting away from Captain Brunt and his awful men.

"Uh um, sir," Captain Brunt called after the man, "might you be interested in this special item I have?"

From his pocket he produced Bonnie's necklace of pearls.

'This indeed would make a wonderful present for my wife,' he thought and they agreed a price.

Bonnie, with her head lowered did not see the transaction.

Holding hands, the man and Bonnie then made their way up the beach.

Chapter Five

New Beginning

As they walked the man spoke to Bonnie and he tried to imagine the feelings of pain and danger she had been through; to have been snatched from her family and brought all this way in an evil smelling ship and treated like an animal, or even worse, with very little food and water, was almost beyond his imagination.

'She is an absolute marvel to have survived.' He thought.

How his own beautiful daughter would have coped having to face such an ordeal he couldn't bear to think of.

The yellow sands gave way to tufts of rough green grass as the odd couple made their way up the rock strewn path to the cobbled cliff road. Bonnie looked around to see if any of the women she had been on the ship with were near, but there was no-one to be seen.

Bonnie's eye's widened, and she stopped in her tracks, as she came face to face with two enormous, unfamiliar creatures, who blew hot steamy saliva from their nostrils and shook their heads at her. She had never before seen a horse. She had once seen a beautiful maned lion being chased off by the warriors as they waved their shields and spears and made threatening cries. She had seen wild boars, monkeys, apes and even a gorilla, which was enormous, but these she had never encountered or seen. She was a little uneasy as the man helped her into the carriage which was attached to these creatures.

"It's safe, I promise you," said the man in a calm, gentle voice, lifting Bonnie into the carriage.

Bonnie felt reassured by his calmness as they then set off along the bumpy bay road to another cove where a large ship was anchored. They stopped and got out of the carriage. The man handed the driver some coins and turned to call to some men waiting on the beach. He took Bonnie by the hand and they walked on the pebbly shingle to the foaming edge of the sea where a brightly painted rowboat was bobbing up and down on the water.

"This child is joining us." Said the man.

"Aye Aye Captain Yelland!" Came the reply

More words were exchanged and it became obvious to Bonnie that this man was in charge and that he was the ship's Captain and the waiting men were some of his crew.

The Captain picked Bonnie up into his arms and waded out to the rowboat. He sat her next to him on the bench. Bonnie started to cry softly as they headed for the large ship, she was afraid that she had misjudged this man, this Captain. What waited for her on board the ship? Another dark 'hole'? Another long and unbearable journey? Should she jump off the boat now and be swept away out to sea? The Captain put his arm around her shoulders. "You're safe, do not cry, this is not the same type of ship." He knew she could not understand his words and he wished he had another form of transportation, as he sensed she was so frightened.

Princess Bonnie looked at the Captain, he was smiling as he spoke and her fears faded.

The rowing boat pulled along side the ship and the Captain, the crew and Bonnie climbed aboard. As they boarded the Captain gave orders and the smartly dressed sailors in their white and blue striped shirts and navy trousers set about securing the rowboat. The anchor was raised and the sails unfurled, the wind caught them and the ship moved on the waves.

The Captain, looking around, asked young Joe, the cabin boy, to bring some food for their new passenger. Joe had been watching as Bonnie came aboard and with Captain Yellands bidding he went to the galley in search of cook, who was not about, so he put together what he thought would be suitable food. Bonnie had been given the small cabin next to Joe's and there, knocking quietly on the door the boy entered and placed, on the little table, in front of this *strange* girl, a plate of bread and cheese, with an apple and a mug of water. Bonnie was so hungry and although reluctant at first she took a quick glance about her, grasped a piece of bread and started to eat. Joe offered her the mug of water and she drank it down. She didn't like the cheese much but she ate it anyway. She liked the apple.

Joe was not much older than Bonnie and they became friends immediately, he was pleased to think she would be with him on this next journey. He imagined they would be able to have great fun together.

In the one corner of the cabin was a hammock for Bonnie to sleep in and after being shown how to use it by Joe, like any seven year old child, she had great fun trying it out! They both laughed as time and again she fell on the floor.

Bonnie was given some of the boy's clothes to wear, they were slightly too big, they were rough and itchy but they kept her warm during the long days and nights.

The Captain spent much time with her trying to find out a little about her and soon it became evident that her name was 'Bonnie' and she in turn learned his name was 'Yelland', although she had difficulty saying this and in her broken speech she called him 'Lelland' which made him and the crew laugh.

Bonnie and Joe had lots of fun together and they spent their spare time playing games of hide and seek and chase. Bonnie learned much from Joe; he was very mischievous and often played tricks on the hard working sailors. He had taught her to call some of the sailor's names, like 'Mr. Baldy' and 'Mr. Lanky' and they laughed as they were chased away by the sailors with their mops. He often marched round wearing one of Captain Yelland's naval caps pretending to be in charge…Bonnie sensed Joe would one day be the captain of his own ship.

Joe was nothing like her beloved friend Bobo but they got on very well and needed no language to understand each other. She copied Joe and helped him with his chores. Life on the ship was teaching her a lot about the white people and she realised that not all white people were to be feared, at least not on this ship.

As time passed, Bonnie became more and more content with her surroundings and began to say more words in English.

The ship's cat, Alfie, was a great favourite with both children. They often saved scraps from their meals to feed to him and he in turn brought them treasures of 'mice'! Some evenings Alfie would jump  onto Bonnie's hammock and would curl up at her feet for the night.

After what had seemed like a whole new lifetime to Bonnie, the ship reached a busy fishing port and Bonnie was astonished by the number of ships in the harbour. One ship was belching out grey black smoke and Bonnie was amazed that it was not on fire. Gulls swooped and screeched all around.

Men sat on the harbour wall mending fishing nets and Bonnie watched many children, with interest, as they rushed around the harbour playing with hoops and skipping ropes.

The sailors lowered the sails and the ship's anchor. They began unloading some special goods for the Queen. Captain Yelland took Bonnie's hand and they, along with a few of the ship's crew went ashore.

Other crew members stayed on board overseeing the unloading; Joe was one of them, he had to stay to help and as Bonnie looked back he was waving vigorously. Tears came into her eyes as this parting reminded her of her separation from Bobo. She stood for a moment and waved back and called his name.

Captain Yelland and Bonnie said goodbye to the men and got into a waiting carriage. The driver stared at Bonnie; he was surprised to see the Captain with a little black girl dressed like a cabin boy!

As they journeyed, Bonnie could hardly believe all the things her eyes were seeing. After leaving the harbour and the sight of all the different boats and ships, she now saw different buildings and there were so many carriages transporting people around the bay. She stared this way and that at all the people and marvelled at how some of the ladies had such big heads; not realising they were wearing very large bonnets! Children ran around in the street shouting and laughing. There were so many questions going around in Bonnie's head but she was unable to ask 'Lelland', so, she sat in the carriage and just looked in wonder.

They travelled on away from the sea and she gazed at the lush green grass and the high hedges. The different animals she saw running in the fields made her gasp and squeal excitedly. The large country houses set back off the road made her eyes light up. Then she recalled her own home…and quietly sat back in her seat.

The coach rattled and bounced as they entered another little town. After a while of travelling the Captain called to the driver to stop. They pulled up outside a gown shop with many pretty clothes hanging in the window. Bonnie and the Captain went inside.

"It's time you had new clothes." He said, and turning to the lady shop keeper he asked her to dress Bonnie in something pretty and appropriate and to choose other pieces of clothing for them to take away. As the lady came toward her, measure in hand, and an armful of clothes, she directed Bonnie to a back room. Bonnie was anxious and she made it quite clear that she didn't want any help and was going to dress herself! Standing aside the shop keeper held out garments one at a time for her to try on, but Bonnie got very frustrated not knowing how to wear them and so accepted the help offered.

Finally dressed to the satisfaction of the shop keeper, but without shoes and stockings, Bonnie approached Captain Yelland. He smiled and held out his hand to her.

Bonnie and the Captain, carrying many packages, got back into the carriage and with the flick of the whip from the driver the carriage with its restless horses, moved off along the bumpy cobbles and out into the countryside once again.

A few miles further on they came to a black and white painted inn and swinging in the wind on the side of the building was a large sign showing a painting of a lion. Bonnie was excited to see something familiar and she pointed through the carriage window.

Captain Yelland looked and said "Yes…It's a Lion." And he held up his hands and made a roaring sound. "Lion." He repeated.

Bonnie laughed. "Lion." She said.

The carriage pulled into the cobbled courtyard and the sea Captain helped Bonnie down. They entered the inn through a large oak door and sat at a wooden table. A large fire burned in the open hearth and a cauldron hung over the flames. The jolly innkeeper came over with a jug of ale and asked what they would like.

Some meat and bread was brought over by a young woman, along with two bowls of steaming broth and a pitcher of water. The broth was very good. Bonnie picked up the bread and began to eat as she watched 'Lelland' use his knife to cut the meat. Bonnie picked up her meat and definitely found her fingers were best. It was how she and Joe had eaten on the ship and how she had eaten at home with her mother and father.

Chapter Six

Meeting Mary

After they were refreshed they left the old inn. Bonnie looked up at the 'Lion' sign still swinging in the wind and she smiled. The coach trundled along the rough road. The evening began to draw in and the moon shone in the clear sky. Bonnie started to fall asleep and Captain Yelland hailed to the driver to stop at the next coaching inn. The carriage entered the large dark courtyard of 'The Wild Boar' and Bonnie sat up with a start. Through the carriage window in the light of the moon she again recognized a familiar animal painted outside the inn.

"That's a 'boar'." said 'Lelland'. "Boar." He made a grunting noise

In her excited tone she repeated. "Boar!" She smiled broadly at him repeating the grunt.

Inside, the inn was dimly lit, the smell of candle wax and wood smoke wafted in the air. They were greeted by the portly landlord and his wife.

Captain Yelland asked that Bonnie be shown to a room for the night and reluctantly she was taken up some wooden stairs by the innkeeper's wife, who carried a small flickering candle in a brass candlestick. The innkeeper's wife was very large, and with each step the wooden boards creaked and flexed under her weight. They entered a little room with a window looking out to where the horses were stabled and the little girl stood and stared for a time, tapping the glass gently and watching the clouds float across the moon. She wondered if it was the same moon that she had seen so many times with her father and mother.

The innkeeper's wife put down the candlestick and looked at Bonnie, she could see that the child was not happy, so she spent time with her pointing out the things in the room.

"This is the bowl you can wash yourself in, and here, in this jug is the water." She picked up the jug and poured water into the bowl and put her hands in and swished them about, then she picked up the towel and wiped them, and handed it to Bonnie - Bonnie knew all this, Joe the cabin boy had been a good teacher, but she could not say so easily, therefore she nodded and said 'yes' a few times. Bonnie looked around the faintly lit room and noticed the large mirror on the wall and was startled by her full reflection. She flicked the skirt of the silk dress she was wearing and ran her hands across the collar and then over her dark curls. She pulled a funny face at herself and jumped up and down, then hid at the side of the mirror and jumped out at herself. The candle made dancing shadows around the room which made her smile.

Her game was interrupted by the innkeeper's wife touching her and pointing to the bed. This was no bed that Bonnie had ever seen. She looked about the room for a hammock, then shrugged her shoulders and sat on the bed. It was very soft and she gave a little bounce on it and for the first time she gave a little sigh of pleasure. The innkeeper's wife gave her a long white garment and signed that she should undress and put it on to sleep in. She pulled back the bedclothes and gestured by slapping the bed for the little girl to climb in. She smiled at Bonnie then made her way out of the room squeezing herself through the small door which shut with a click of the latch. Bonnie ran to the door and flicked the latch to open it - it squeaked as she pulled back the door and she furtively peeped out. She could hear a lot of talking and laughing but was unable to see past the first few steps and only the yellow light from an oil lamp downstairs reflecting on the ceiling was visible. Bonnie shut the door gently and got into the bed without taking any of her clothes off. The bed was so soft and warm that she was asleep in seconds.

The candle flickered and died.

Early next morning the innkeeper's wife entered the child's room and gave her a gentle shake which made Bonnie sit up quickly. The innkeeper's wife gave a little laugh when she saw that the child was fully dressed in bed; she again showed Bonnie all the things to do, after which she led Bonnie downstairs where breakfast was set out. 'Lelland' was sitting at the table waiting, and he smiled at her and pointed for her to sit down to eat. They ate fruit, porridge and oatcakes with a mug of milk to wash it down. It was a good meal which Bonnie enjoyed.

The coach was waiting at the front of the inn with fresh horses for the journey. They travelled on and the light began to fail as they approached the city where trees and grass gave way to cobbles and stone. Bonnie again marvelled at all the things she saw; the houses were lit up brightly and streams of coloured light filtered through the windows.

The coach and horses pulled in through a large gateway and up a winding drive and in front of them was an extremely large stone house. As the coach came to a stop at the front entrance, light seemed to stream from everywhere.

"This is 'Deerpark House'," Captain Yelland said to Bonnie.

Although she did not understand it then, it was a place she would come to love.

A little girl of about five came running down the steps as the seaman got out of the coach. "Papa, Papa," she called, "you are home at last. Mama and I thought you would never come back."

A tall pretty lady stood behind the child.

"Have you brought me a present Papa?" The little fair headed girl asked.

"Of course I have my darling," he said. "I have brought you *many* presents and something *special* for Mama."

He leaned over and kissed the tall pretty lady and kissed the little girl on the head.

"What have you brought for me Papa?" The child continued eagerly.

"Well, your presents are in my luggage, but I also have a special surprise for you."

"Let me see, let me see." The child was excited.

The sea Captain leaned back into the coach and took Bonnie by the hand and helped her down the steps. The little fair headed girl took several paces backwards. A look of confusion spread across her face.

Mary, the Captain's daughter, stood with her back against her mother. "Who is that?" she asked pulling her head and body sideways. "Why she is all dirty? I have never seen anyone with such a dirty face and hands".

"No darling, she is not dirty, this is Bonnie, she is just a little older than you are and she has come from a very very hot country where everyone is this colour so that their skin does not burn in the hot sunshine."

"I don't like her. Do you like her Mama?" The little girl with her big blue eyes looked up, but her mother said nothing.

Bonnie did not understand any of the words, but she did understand that this little girl did not like her and she gripped the Captain's hand very tightly as she looked up at him and said "No 'Lelland'… 'Lelland' no." And she pulled back behind him.

"What is she calling you Papa?" The little girl was laughing.

"Mary, she is only just learning to talk our language, you must be patient with her, she is very clever and she will soon be able to talk to us properly."

"I don't like her," was Mary's reply, and she turned her back and ran up the steps into the house.

The sea Captain, with Bonnie and his wife followed Mary into the beautiful drawing room, with its huge pictures on the walls and a large mirror over a glowing crackling fire.

"What *good* presents did you bring me Papa?" The little girl asked. "The ones that you have in your luggage?" The little blue eyed girl looked up at her father with an enchanting smile and his heart melted.

"They will be a surprise for tomorrow my darling."

"Please Papa, please." The sea Captain picked up his daughter and hugged her.

"Tomorrow Mary."

"Well, if I can't have *my* presents right now, what did you bring for Mama?"

The Captain put his daughter down and pulled from his pocket the beautiful set of pearls, that hung with the golden emblem and the one black pearl at the centre, and held them for his wife to see.

"Oh!" she exclaimed "It is the most beautiful necklace that I have ever seen."

Bonnie's eyes widened and she held out her hand.

"Oh! Look Mama, she wants your pearls." Laughed Mary.

Bonnie shrank back behind 'Lelland', so that no one would see the tears in her eyes.

He spoke to his wife very quietly. "My darling," he said, "I happened to be on the beach when this pirate slave ship was unloading its *human cargo,* and I saw this child, she looked so bewildered, unhappy and so frail, I felt that I had to help her." He took his wife's hand and looked at her, but she said nothing. "The pirate, Captain Brunt told me that she is a *Princess,* the daughter of a King and Queen of a tribe from a far off land. To be snatched from her family and taken in a loathsome slave ship across the sea to a strange place and to even stranger people…. Well, I felt I could not leave her to the mercy of a slave master."

His wife looked up at him and said, "You are a wonderful man, and of course I understand you bringing her here, she is still only an infant. We shall look after her and she can be educated with Mary, and when she is older we can find her suitable employment.

"Yes Mama," Mary interrupted, "I don't like her, we can make her work in our kitchen."

For Bonnie, the sea Captain's house was far beyond anything she had or could ever have imagined. The life that she had had with her father and mother had been wonderful - but *this place* and the things that she saw were things that she could never have dreamed of. The food, the clothes, the animals, the books, the rooms, light when it was dark, not just fire light or moon light, but little shiny lamps that would fill a dark room with light, all these things were way beyond her comprehension. This place was so interesting and wonderful, but, she would have gladly left it to be with her mother and father in her village and to see and play with her best friend Bobo again.

Chapter Seven

Life at Deerpark House

For her young years, Bonnie was very wise, and her thoughts were that she must get on with her life as it was now. Her family and her past would always be with her and she thought that one day she may even be able to return home, but as things were, she would make the best of her situation and learn as much as she could.

Bonnie was not particularly keen on wearing the masses of clothes put out for her, where she had lived was always hot and a thin floral cloth wrapped around and tied at the top had been comfortable to wear, but here the weather was not so hot, and sometimes thick clothes were necessary, but it took a long time for her to get used to them and she had almost preferred the itchy cabin boys shirt and trousers, but those clothes were not befitting a young lady, she had been told by 'Lelland'. She did however like the pretty bonnet and wore them whenever possible.

One morning she woke to a blanket of white snow covering the ground. She gasped and ran downstairs into the kitchen passed cook and the kitchen staff and out through the door. She stopped abruptly when her feet touched the cold wet snow and she squealed. Cook, who was a little on the large size, chased after her as fast as she was able and laughed at the sight of the little girl, in her nightdress and *bonnet* standing in the snow in her bare feet, with arms outstretched catching the snowflakes and looking in wonder as they melted on the palms of her hands.

Cook chuckled, "This is 'snow'. It comes from the sky during wintertime, in the wintertime we have a very special celebration called 'Christmas' and tomorrow is Christmas Day!" Cook reached for Bonnie and pulled her into the steamy kitchen and shut the door. "When you are dressed in your warm clothes you can go out to play in the snow, it will be great fun!" Cook motioned to Bonnie by pulling at her nightdress and said, "Go and get dressed."

Bonnie didn't understand many of the words Cook said as she spoke so fast, but she realised that Cook had been pointing at the glistening flakes that were falling from the sky. She once more tried to open the back door and took little notice of Cook as she repeated the word 'Snow' several times.

Cook turned Bonnie toward the stairs. Bonnie, hurried out of the warm kitchen into the dimly lit hall and up the stairs. She ran up several steps before she noticed a glow coming from the partially opened sitting room door. She stopped, crouched and peeped through the banisters and saw something so pretty that it made her gasp with delight. She began to back slowly down the stairs one step at a time keeping her eyes firmly fixed on what she could see. She moved slowly across the cold marble hall floor toward the sight. When she reached the large door she pushed it wide open and stared in amazement. She turned quickly and saw Captain Yellend and his wife standing by the fire looking at her. She looked again at the beautiful sight in the corner of the room. An enormous green tree stood there covered in glittering, sparkling streamers and shiny round twinkling balls that changed colour as the glowing firelight was reflected in them. The tree branches had also been covered in white and silver dust which looked like 'frosty snow'. She gave a further gasp and rushed up to the tree and touched the white dust and said 'snow', but it was not cold and wet like the other snow and it did not melt on her hand. Captain Yelland beckoned to her to come over and warm herself by the fire. She made her way across the room not taking her eyes off the tree. There were so many questions she wanted to ask. 'Why was the tree *in* the room?' 'Why was it covered in sparkly things?' and 'What were those pretty things underneath?'

At this moment Mary came into the room removing her hat, scarf and gloves and tossing them onto the floor for Nanny to pick up.

Mary looked at Bonnie who was still staring at the huge Christmas tree.

"What is she doing Mama and *what* is she saying? Why isn't she dressed properly?" Mary pointed. "Look, she has her nightclothes on back to front! And what has she got on her head?" Mary gave a little laugh, "She does look a frightful mess. I don't want her touching my presents Mama. I don't suppose she's even heard of Father Christmas! Do you think she knows about Father Christmas Papa? Do you think Father Christmas knows she's here? Will he bring her any presents Papa?"

"I don't suppose Mary…" her father paused, "that Bonnie has ever celebrated Christmas as we do. Everything here is very different and very new to Bonnie, but I know she will soon learn about our ways. We must make her welcome and help her to adjust and understand, and I am sure Father Christmas will know she is here and bring her some presents of her own!"

Mary shrugged her shoulders. "Make sure she doesn't take any of my presents from under the tree, won't you Mama?"

Nanny pulled on Mary's arm and they left the sitting room and made their way upstairs to the nursery. Bonnie was collected by one of the maids and struggling, she was taken to her room to dress properly, ready for her snowy adventure outside.

Mary looking back said, "She is naughty isn't she Nanny?"

Nanny looked at Mary and smiled.

Time passed and despite Mary, Bonnie was to experience many happy Christmas times at Deerpark House with 'Lelland'.

For Bonnie the months flew by at an unbelievable pace. Every morning, except Sunday, at nine o'clock sharp she went to private language lessons. The tutor was amazed at how quickly she learned. She would then join Mary for sewing, music or painting lessons and as a pupil she was very apt, especially at music. This made Mary hate her all the more, and she would make trouble for her whenever she had the opportunity; she hid things and blamed Bonnie for taking them, she broke things and again blamed Bonnie, and although the tutors were sympathetic to Bonnie, they were, if confronted, inclined to side with Mary as she was the 'young lady' of the house.

Bonnie was now thirteen, having been with the family for a little over five years. She was growing into a lovely and most intelligent young woman, softly spoken and polite with impeccable manners. Bonnie held herself as any Princess should, tall and straight. Her long and wavy, shiny black hair was always neatly plaited and held to one side with a silk ribbon tied in a large bow.

She was now able to speak, read and write her new language with ease and until recently she had always been reluctant to relate her story, but she knew she could explain to 'Lelland' the many things that had happened to her. She told him about the King and Queen - her father and mother - and of the tribe, how they lived, how they hunted, what they ate. She told him about Bobo, her best friend, the fun they had together and how they were captured by the hated and fearful neighbouring tribal Chief. "Bobo promised to rescue me," she said, " he must have been captured himself…" her face saddened. She was here, with 'Lelland' who provided everything she could possibly wish for, but she still felt hurt not knowing Bobo's fate. She so wanted to know he was well. He would always be in her heart.

The one thing that she did not tell the Captain, was the name her father used to call her; she was his 'Little Black Pearl', and she never told that the beautiful pearl necklace 'Lelland' had given to his wife was indeed hers, stolen from her by the fearful Chief when she had been captured.

The Captain listened with great interest to all she had to say. He told her that she should write down everything that she could remember.

They discussed the slave trade that had brought her to this place and he explained to her. "Bonnie, it is a dreadful thing that happened to you. Now, slavery in many parts of the world has been abolished and I hope you understand that the slave ship you were on was doing wrong." He hesitated. "I was not able to stop them, and I am only pleased that I was able to rescue you from Captain Brunt."

"I am very pleased too. It is nice to be here with you. I think I might have died if you had not saved me. Thank you Captain 'Lelland'." Although she was able to speak his name properly now, she still called him 'Lelland'.

Bonnie hugged 'Lelland' and he gave her a little tickle as she did so, which made her giggle.

Mary had been watching her father and Bonnie together and she hated their closeness. She was a very spoilt child and despised Bonnie more and more every day, especially for calling her father 'Lelland', which irritated her intensely, and the thought that Bonnie was actually a *Princess* upset her so much that she continually said nasty things about her and did everything she could to discredit her with her father. Most everyone in the house knew how Mary disliked Bonnie, she had made no secret of it since that first evening when her father had brought Bonnie into their home. She had never even tried to like her. There seemed to be no way of making her change her attitude.

Bonnie would have liked to be friends with Mary. She had never hurt Mary and they were similar in age. Bonnie did not want to steal 'Lelland' away. She had, once, tried to explain all of this to Mary, but Mary had not wanted to listen and had shouted at Bonnie how much she hated her and definitely *did not* want her in her home.

Nevertheless, Bonnie learned all her lessons well and had many conversations with the numerous visitors that frequented the sea Captain's house. She became something of a celebrity; they all loved to hear her childlish stories of the dark continent. By now she had also mastered several musical instruments and the visitors loved to hear her play the pianofortè.

Despite the sea Captains endeavours, Mary's hatred for Bonnie grew, and it was obvious that Bonnie should move on, as she was now an accomplished child able to read and write and communicate well, but she hated the thought of leaving 'Deerpark House'.

Captain Yelland knew many suitable households who were only too willing to take Bonnie under their wing, she was still very young but would make a favourable member to any household. At thirteen she was a very pleasant and capable child.

Captain Yelland had already spoken to Bonnie of his concerns for her future, and so he explained that she was to meet with the Duke and Duchess of Morechester who needed a companion for their young daughter, Clara, who was also thirteen. Bonnie had seen Clara on several occasions, when the Duke and Duchess had visited 'Deerpark House' and she liked her very much, but she was greatly distressed at the thought of having to leave the protection of her wonderful Captain, as he and his wife had cared for her for many years and she loved them dearly. She appreciated all the things he had done for her and all the friends she had met within *his* household. It was only the attitude of Mary that had sometimes made her life there so very miserable.

Captain Yelland arranged for Bonnie to meet the Duke and Duchess. The fact that she was going as a friend to the daughter of the house would mean that she actually would be joining more as a family member than just a companion.

It troubled Bonnie to think that she may not see kind 'Lelland' for a long time, but she put it out of her mind and began to look forward to staying with Clara.

Chapter Eight

Morechester Manor

So it was that one fine morning, when she was dressed in her finest white dress with its many lacy petticoats, and with her long black hair neatly adorned with pretty ribbons, that she was officially to meet the Duke and Duchess of Morechester Manor and their daughter Clara.

A carriage was waiting at the front of the house as Captain Yelland and Bonnie walked down the steps, and, at that moment the sun began to shine brightly and Bonnie thought that it was a good omen for her. A footman opened the door of the carriage and the two got in. Bonnie sat on the one side and 'Lelland' sat opposite, and he could sense her unease… he smiled and tried to calm her fears.

"You will like the Duke and Duchess," he said. "They are very kind and generous people, and Clara is a fine young lady too, just your age."

The carriage trundled through the busy streets and out into the countryside. The road now began to zig zag this way and that around hills and trees and it became very bumpy. The sun was now blazing down and there were people collecting the sun dried yellow hay and forking it on to the high sided horse drawn carts. Bonnie loved the countryside, the sun dried fields reminded her of her homeland.

Soon the carriage was entering the small market town of Morechester and the road surface had changed from clay to cobbles, they passed many small black and white cottages on either side of the road and then the horses were pulled up in front of a set of enormous iron gates. Up the drive set off to the right Bonnie could see a small lake with some herons standing by the low shrubs against the edge of the water. The carriage passed through an avenue of trees which held back some of the sunshine, then the tall poplars gave way to ornamental flowering trees and shrubs. The grand house came into view, it was large and impressive, and nothing like 'Lellands'. The carriage stopped outside the huge front porch with its large stone pillars and eight steps that led to the carved oak door, and before the foot man had opened the carriage door the butler had emerged from the house and was at the bottom porch step ready to meet them.

Captain Yelland was a frequent visitor to the house, and the butler greeted them both warmly. He led them into the vast hall with its stained glass windows and imposing staircase. There were many doors leading from the hallway and the butler led the two guests through to the drawing room where the Duke and Duchess were waiting.

"James," smiled the Duke, "come in and sit down….. and *this*, of course is Bonnie."

Bonnie made her best curtsy, and both the Duke and the Duchess held out their hand to her.

"You will be a fine friend for Clara, she gets a little lonely out here all by herself. She is having a music lesson at the moment. Do sit down child."

Bonnie obeyed, and so began another chapter in her life.

Clara was nothing like Mary, she was a very cheerful and kind young girl, and she and Bonnie became the best of friends immediately – truth be to tell, Clara had played with Mary on many occasions and she had found her very hard to get along with; Mary did not like sharing her things and when they played games Mary always had to win, but with Bonnie, things were totally different. Bonnie and Clara were to have many happy times together.

The Duke and Duchess brought in the best tutors for the two girls. Bonnie found learning much more enjoyable as lessons along side Clara were great fun.

Most people who came into contact with Bonnie thought her to be a remarkable child, she had learned to speak the language perfectly and was outstanding at most things. She certainly excelled at music and the Duke and Duchess and their friends loved to hear her and Clara playing duets on the piano. Bonnie's paintings too, were excellent, she painted many scenes of the home she remembered before she was cruelly snatched away – she drew likeness' of her Father and

Mother and of the tribesmen all dressed in their hunting array with their shields and spears, and she drew pictures of Bobo the friend she could not forget. She painted scenes of the plateau with its magnificent waterfall, and in her darker moments she painted pictures of the slave ship with its prisoners and guards. Clara loved the stories that Bonnie told her, and she loved the paintings that Bonnie did and so she persuaded her father the Duke to allow Bonnie's paintings to be displayed around the great hall.

Time went very fast, and the girls were now seventeen. They were fine young ladies.

Clara and Bonnie had great times helping in the household, they loved to spend time in the kitchen, baking. They were never too proud to help with the chores. They were both liked by all the staff. Bonnie became a favourite with the female members of staff as she often passed on the clothes she no longer needed. The male workers enjoyed her stories, and she liked to draw pictures of them at their work.

Morechester was not far from the sea, and with permission from the Duke, the girls, with their tutors, often made trips to the coastal areas where they loved to explore and discover new things. They loved the sandy beaches and the harbour, where they watched the fishermen mending their nets and gazed at the sailing and steam ships. They also loved their trips out into the country where they could have picnics by the river and paint scenes of the landscape. Growing up at Morechester Manor was a lovely time for Bonnie although she still missed 'Lelland' and thought of him always, especially when she was at the seaside, as it brought to mind that fateful day on the beach when he had saved her from certain misery.

Bonnie saw 'Lelland' occasionally as he sometimes used the harbour just outside Morechester when he returned from his sailing expeditions. As he was so close to the Duke and Duchess' home he would visit and he and Bonnie would spend time together, and would walk round the grounds of the estate - she loved these days.

Captain Yelland, who was a Captain in Her Majesty's Navy made frequent visits to see The Queen at the Castle to report on naval matters. He was a great favourite of the Her Majesty, and they had long discussions regarding his seafaring adventures, especially his success in seizing many pirates ships.

The Queen had an alternative motive for inviting Captain Yelland to the Castle on this day.

"I have a special reason for asking you here today, James." She paused. "I wish to discuss with you your future in my navy. It is with the greatest pleasure that I call upon you to become The Admiral of the Fleet and you are to take charge of my new vessel 'Windward'. She is a grand ship!"

Captain Yelland was astounded. He had no idea of the Queen's intention. "Your Majesty, I am overwhelmed."

"It is only what you deserve, you have served me well over these past years." She smiled at him.

"Thank you, Your Majesty." He replied.

"Your ship, The 'Pearlstar' and crew are now to be captained by Mr Hamley."

"Mr. Hamley! A fine young man. He will make a splendid Captain." Yelland nodded.

The Queen did not dwell on Captain Yellands new appointment and she continued. "Tell me of the progress of the young slave girl you rescued from that dreadful pirate slave ship."

"Bonnie is now eighteen, your Majesty, she is very bright and very clever, she adjusted well to her new life. She excels at most things and she loves music and painting. She has suffered much in her short life, losing her mother, father and all her friends to the slave trade, but she has come through the trials with great tenacity."

"I wonder," The Queen paused, "if there is anything we can do to find Bonnie's father and mother, if indeed they have survived!"

"That would be wonderful for Bonnie, but, I fear, not an easy thing to achieve."

" 'We' will have to see what 'We' can do." She responded.

Captain Yelland continued. "At present Bonnie is living with the Duke and Duchess of Morechester at their country residence, and she has made an excellent companion for Clara their daughter."

"Yes, Clara, lovely girl," replied the Queen, "and I shall look forward to meeting Bonnie and Clara with the Duke and Duchess at the Ball to be held here at the castle next week. Of course, you and your beautiful wife and your charming daughter Mary are also expected to join in the fun."

"Thank you, your Majesty, I know Mary is very much looking forward to the Ball."

The Queen, although busy with many state matters, was very fond of James Yelland and they talked on for sometime.

Bonnie and Clara were indeed looking forward to the Ball at the castle. Bonnie had never met the

Queen and when Clara told her that they would be presented to Her Majesty, Bonnie was a little hesitant.

"She won't bite you." Clara said with a little giggle. "Shall we go and choose our dresses for the Ball?" Hand in hand the girls ran up the carved staircase to their dressing room.

Chapter Nine

The Grand Ball

The night of the Ball came, and a fine carriage glowing with many lights waited at the front door for the Duke, Duchess and the two exquisitely dressed young ladies. They were helped to their seats by a finely dressed footman, their silk dresses rustling and shimmering in the moonlight. They pulled blankets over their knees. The Duke and Duchess sat opposite them and gave last minute instructions on how to approach the Queen. The bright moon was shining and stars twinkled, making the coach driver's journey easy as there was not a cloud in the sky.

The journey to the Castle took quite a time. The coach laboured through the near empty, steep bumpy streets and then they were out into the countryside. When they arrived at their destination, the large ornate iron gates were manned by two guards. Looking through the carriage window, Bonnie could see the magnificent stone battlements, and she could just make out guards walking back and forth at the top of them as the moonlight glinted on their helmets. She could make out fine lawns on both sides of the drive, with ornamental trees and shrubs decorating the way. Burning torches around the arched entrance to the castle made a magnificent sight. They drove over a cobbled slope and across the moat draw-bridge. The portcullis had been raised and they entered a huge courtyard ringed with stone pillars ablaze with more flaming torches.

Many carriages had already arrived and their occupants were making their way to an enormous carved oak door at which stood two guards with long crossed spears. Sparkling light shone out through the door casting their long shadows.

Their carriage pulled up near the entrance and with the help of the footman the four alighted and as she did so, Bonnie could see 'Lelland' with his family. Mary, with her long golden hair, looked so beautiful, and Bonnie shrank back a little as she was beginning to feel a slightly anxious. She wished 'Lelland' could have been with her. Clara was there and she understood Bonnie's fears, and held her hand.

A chubby red faced courtier, dressed in fine clothes, greeted them at the entrance to the ballroom and announced the names from a card he was handed.

"The Duke and Duchess of Morechester Manor, with Miss Clara and Miss Bonnie."

They entered the magnificent ballroom. Then Bonnie heard the courtier call… "Admiral Yelland, Mrs. Harriet Yelland with their daughter Miss Mary."

Bonnie stood rooted to the spot for a moment. 'Admiral' she repeated quietly and smiled proudly.

Bonnie had no more time to think as she and Clara were directed to walk up the red carpet to where the Queen was sitting on a large golden throne. Out of the corner of her eye, Bonnie could see large portraits of fine ladies and gentlemen hanging on the walls, but she dared not look at them, she kept her eyes looking straight in front of her. They came to a stepped area where the grand throne was occupied by a distinguished looking lady in the most magnificent dress that Bonnie had ever seen; it was of fine white silk embroidered with gold thread, it was low on the neck with tiers of frills on the sleeves which reached a little below her elbows, it had a long train which folded at her feet and she wore a royal blue sash over one shoulder. A crimson cape edged with ermine draped loosely and touched the floor. Her black hair, back off her face, was in a tight chignon, and she wore a jewelled crown and long golden earrings that matched her golden necklace. She wore golden shoes on her feet and they rested on a crimson and gold footstool.

Bonnie looked in amazement and wonder. *'This is the Queen.'* She thought to herself. Clara gave a little tug on her arm and the spell was broken; she took her cue from Clara and gave her finest curtsy.

The Queen studied both girls and in turn she asked them to step forward. She beckoned to Clara to come forward first and Clara mounted the step and curtsied again. Her Majesty knew Clara quite well and spoke to her about Morechester things, and she wanted to know how she was getting on in her studies.

Now it was Bonnie's turn, "Come forward child". Bonnie mounted the step and curtsied again. "You are eighteen years old now child, is that correct?"

"Yes your Majesty" she replied. The Queen spent several minutes speaking to Bonnie before the two girls were able to back down and continue onto the dance floor. Bonnie looked around and saw that Mary was now talking to the Queen. But she couldn't see any sign of 'Lelland'.

Then Bonnie felt a hand touch her shoulder and there he was.

"Will you put me down on your dance card for the next waltz?" he asked.

Bonnie smiled. "Yes, *Admiral*." And she did so.

They were then interruped by Mary. She pulled on his arm. "Come on father, this is my dance." She said, but she said nothing to Bonnie.

The Admiral and Mary spun away joining in a long line of other dancers but he looked back and said, "The next waltz". Bonnie smiled and nodded, and gave a little wave.

Soon Bonnie was surrounded by admiring young men all booking a dance with her, and she wrote their names on her dance card. Clara had been dancing with her father and she had now come over to Bonnie, and she too was surrounded by romantic admirers.

"Isn't this fun Bonnie?" Clara said, "I could dance all night long."

Just at that point Mary came up to them, "Hello Clara, it is wonderful, isn't it? Do you know my father is an Admiral now?"

Clara smiled.

Mary went on…"Look, my dance card is full. I have the next dance booked with that handsome officer, William Miles, you know, William *Thomas* Miles. Son of the Marquis of Longthorne. Have you danced with him yet?"

"Not yet, though both Bonnie and I have a dance booked with him." Mary turned and walked away with her nose in the air.

The evening went very swiftly, Bonnie had had her dance with Admiral 'Lelland' and many fine young men. Now the Ball was over, the journey home began.

"It was a lovely evening Bonnie, wasn't it?" Clara then turned to the Duke, "The Queen looked so beautiful; she asked me all about Morechester father, and she loved Bonnie." The girls chattered excitedly on their way back to Morechester and Bonnie noticed how Clara's cheeks were a little flushed. Clara sat back in the carriage and closed her eyes, as did Bonnie, who still felt sad that Mary's attitude to her had not changed.

Chapter Ten

Clara Finds Romance

Bonnie and Clara were inseparable, enjoying every minute they were together, and although they each had their own room they often shared just one and sat up late into the night talking about things that made them giggle and chatting about their favourite subjects! Clara's main topic was William Thomas Miles, and she could not help telling how handsome she thought him and how distinguished she thought he looked in his dress uniform. Bonnie agreed that he was indeed very handsome.

At The Ball they both had had many admirers and Clara pressed Bonnie to tell which young man, out of those she danced with, she had liked best. But she could not, although she had been introduced to, and had danced with many of her own countrymen, who like her, had been rescued from the slave trade, she could only say that she felt no excitement or enthusiasm for any of them. Clara continued to press Bonnie for an answer, but yet again Bonnie could only talk of Bobo, the boy she could not forget.

Bonnie thought of Bobo often, her heart yearned to see him again. On that ill-fated day many years before when she had been captured, he had called to her that he '*would find her*', and the words just rang and rang in her ears. '*I **will** find you – I **will** find you*' – Bobo was all that she could think about, she dreamed of him sailing a ship to this land and searching the towns and countryside for her. She imagined the way he would now look, handsome and slim, dressed in fine clothes. How tall would he be? But for all her imaginings, he was not here, he had never found her. Did he remember his promise? Did he even remember her? Was he unable to fulfil his promise? Was he alive? Some days Bonnie would have to stop herself daydreaming of Bobo. She was extremely happy now and she felt privileged and fortunate to have had such a good life.

One afternoon a little while after the Ball, William Thomas Miles had called at Morechester Manor on the pretext of returning Clara's gloves, and he was cordially invited to stay for afternoon tea, after which, Clara and William walked in the rose garden and sat talking for a long while.

The romance between Clara and William blossomed and soon a grand wedding was arranged and was to take place at Morechester Manor. With Bonnie as chief bridesmaid, she and Clara had great fun looking at gown patterns and choosing their favourites. The seamstress flitted around them pinning material here and cutting there, making up the most beautiful gowns.

The wedding day dawned bright and beautiful and the ceremony was a splendid affair and it was here at Clara's wedding reception that Admiral Yelland and his wife together with Mary, walked around the great hall admiring the paintings hung there. It was also here that they saw some of Bonnie's paintings, many of which depicted her childhood days with her father and mother, with scenes of warriors in full tribal dress.

"Bonnie is indeed a gifted artist," said Harriet Yelland to her husband, "see this beautiful waterfall, the many animals and look how she captures the faces of the warrior's in this painting, and the detail on their shields." She paused and leaned forward. "I have seen this emblem somewhere before, I just cannot think where."

Her thoughts were broken by Mary, who had seen enough of Bonnie's paintings and pulling on her father's arm, she insisted. "Let us go into the ballroom and join the dancers."

It was a memorable occasion for Bonnie but one of mixed emotions, as she was happy for Clara but now she felt alone again, Clara was gone - what would become of her now? It seemed to Bonnie that everyone she had ever loved had all been taken from her, there was her mother and father, Bobo, Joe, 'Lelland' and now Clara.

Bonnie felt that her life was like a book with many different chapters, and now at eighteen, she was about to embark on another one.

Chapter Eleven

Reunited

Admiral Yelland went to see the Duke and Duchess of Morechester regarding Bonnie, and they discussed at length her future.

"With Clara now married and living many miles away, it is time for Bonnie to move on too." The Duke said, and he continued. "Clara has told me that Bonnie has many admirers amongst her own countrymen, some are doing very well for themselves, but she doesn't seem to give heed to any of them, it would be well if we could find her a suitable marriage partner."

"It would indeed," replied Admiral Yelland, "but Bonnie has a determined mind of her own, and I think we will be hard pressed to find her someone she can truly love. It seems she still yearns for someone from her past. Meanwhile the position of governess to the two young boys of the Viscount of Westcastle has arisen, and it would be a good opportunity for Bonnie."

All concerned agreed that Bonnie was the ideal person to take up such a position, and so it was, with a heavy heart, that Bonnie went to join the family of the Viscount and Viscountess of Westcastle at Westcastle Court.

The Duke and Duchess of Morechester were quite sad to see Bonnie leave there home, they appreciated the companionship that she had afforded to their daughter Clara, and they trusted that her new post as governess to Samuel and Harry would prove beneficial.

Samuel was five and Harry was four, they were two happy healthy mischievous children. They were slightly taken aback when they first encountered Bonnie but they soon grew to accept and trust her. Bonnie was responsible for keeping the boys happy and entertained. She taught the boys many things and they had great fun learning simple tunes on the piano. They enjoyed many nature walks around the vast gardens and loved the art lessons that she gave them and the stories she told them.

Bonnie was grateful that she always had Sunday afternoons to herself. On one such afternoon she settled herself in the church at Westcastle. The service began and a guest speaker was announced. Bonnie's attention was immediately drawn to a young man sitting at the front of the church, but she could not see his face clearly. The church was dimly lit and she studied him with great interest as he rose from his seat and made his way to the pulpit.

The young man was tall and handsome and he began his story by telling of missionaries travelling to his land, teaching their faith, and how he had been converted to Christianity. In his talk he gave a fascinating account of his home life. He spoke of the wonderful time of his boyhood and the sadness when many of his people were seized by a neighbouring tribe and taken and sold by them for slaves. He explained about his King and Queen being lost and how with the help of his Princess he had escaped. Bonnie was spellbound; his story reminded her so much of the early life that she remembered.

After the service she asked if she could meet with the speaker as his story had captivated her.

Gentle sunlight glistened through magnificent stained glass windows making coloured mosaic shapes on the church walls, as Bonnie waited for the speaker.

She studied the face of the tall black handsome man that walked toward her, and she imagined that she could see in his eyes the little boy that she had known many years before.

She extended her hand. "I am pleased to meet you." She said quietly.

He looked straight at her as he took her hand not letting it go, he too studied her face. "Bonnie! Is it...... you? After all these years, have I at last found you?"

Bonnie's eyes widened and her heart raced. It was not her imagination after all! She flung her arms around his neck. "Bobo. Bobo." Tears of joy streamed down her cheeks. "I have dreamed of this day since our parting so long ago."

"I have prayed to find you." Bobo said, stepping back to look at her. "You have grown into the most beautiful woman I have ever seen."

They walked and talked for a very long time until each had to go their own way. They promised to write to each other and they would meet as often as Bobo's schedule would allow.

Bonnie was so excited she could hardly wait to tell 'Lelland' of the chance meeting with her long lost childhood friend, Bobo, and how he was now a Christian preacher. So she wrote to him immediately on returning to Westcastle Court and he was extremely pleased to receive her news and he wondered if, at last, she had found the man she wanted to marry.

At Bonnie's request, Admiral Yelland called at the Court as soon as he could.

"Bobo has been looking for me for all these years. He never stopped once. Everywhere he travelled he looked for me." She said excitedly. "I am so happy. He is everything I imagined him to be."

"You really love Bobo, don't you ?"

"Oh yes, I do 'Lelland', I really do." She answered.

"Then I should like to meet him, he sounds like a fine fellow."

"Oh! He is…he is, I know you will like him. He is coming back here to Westcastle next week, shall we come over to see you then?"

"Excellent…Please bring him to see us as soon as possible."

"Thank you 'Lelland'. I know you will like and approve of him. We shall visit as soon as he returns."

So it was that Admiral Yelland was at last to meet with the boy that he had heard so much about, and with Bonnie by his side, Bobo spoke to the Admiral relating his story – "After the slave hunt when Princess Bonnie was captured and the King and Queen lost, all the tribe's people that had escaped the wicked Chief came back to their homes and rebuilt everything. I was still young at this time. They guarded the perimeter to keep the slavers out and the tribe set up a council to rule. When I was older they decided that they needed someone to govern them and elected me, just until such time that the King and Queen or Princess Bonnie came back. I did what I could with the help of the tribe's council, and we have had many years of peace."

He paused in his story, and Admiral Yelland urged him to continue. "A missionary visited our tribe and taught us many things of your culture. We learned to speak your language and were taught Christianity. We all became Christians and with the help of the missionary it was decided by the tribe's council that I should go in search of the King and Queen and Princess Bonnie. I have travelled to many lands telling my story. I have looked for Bonnie at every place and I despaired at ever finding her. To find her safe and so well is all that I have wished for."

Bonnie gripped his hand tightly, smiling up at him. "Bonnie has told me how you saved her from the slave master, and looked after her for all those years when she was growing up. I feel, that without her father, the King, being here, *you,* Admiral Yelland as her father figure, should be the person I ask for permission to take Bonnie's hand in marriage."

Admiral Yelland liked Bobo and felt privileged by his request, and without hesitation he agreed.

Chapter Twelve

From This Day Forward

With her husband away with his regiment, Clara, Bonnie's best friend was eager to help with all the wedding preparations. Clara was able to move back to Morchester Manor for a few weeks so that she could be near Bonnie and she was delighted to be asked to be Matron of Honour. Bonnie left her position at Westcastle and moved back to Admiral Yelland's house, where he and his wife would help prepare for the big day. Fortunately Mary was away at finishing school, and would not be back until just before the wedding.

The wedding was certainly going to be a grand affair. Admiral Yelland was to give Bonnie away, and he arranged that open carriages with pairs of white horses would take the main bridal party to the church. The reception would be held in the grand dining room and cook, who felt very proud, would prepare a meal fit for a Princess. Many guests were to be invited.

Bonnie had missed Clara, and now, here they were together again making great plans for Bonnie's wedding. Yards of silk material in white for the bride and pink for Clara and the little bridesmaids was purchased. Little bridesmaids who were very fidgety were dressed and re-dressed by the seamstress. Clara tried to teach them what they should do at the wedding. Samuel and Harry, were to be pageboys and they had great fun dressing up in their blue and white sailor suits and marching around playing on tin whistles.

At last the great day arrived, and the bride looked breathtaking in her white silk dress with a white crushed velvet bodice that was laced with ribbon. There were tiny white pearls sewn along the flowing edges of the sleeves, veil and hem. On her head she wore a beautiful pearl tiara that held a long lace veil in place.

Around her neck, once again, was the pearl necklace with the golden emblem and the shining black pearl!

The Admiral's wife had recognised the golden emblem from Bonnie's paintings of the warrior's shields that were displayed at Morechester Manor and so she had returned the necklace in time for the wedding.

Admiral Yelland, with Clara, the four little bridesmaids, and pageboys Samuel and Harry waited together at the bottom of the fine staircase for the bride to appear.

There were gasps of wonderment from the

guests and staff alike, as Bonnie descended the stairs.

She took 'Lelland's' arm, and he could feel her trembling, he smiled to reassure her. Clara directed two of the little bridesmaids to take up Bonnie's train, the other bridesmaids and the two pageboys joined the procession. 'Lelland' led Bonnie to their waiting carriage which was garlanded with sweet scented oriental lilies. Clara, the little bridesmaids and the pageboys were in the second carriage followed by other carriages making up the entourage.

Outside, at the church, a waiting crowd cheered as the carriages passed through the gates and stopped at the church porch. The bells rang out joyfully. The footmen moved quickly into position to assist the bride and Admiral Yelland from the carriage. Clara and the children took up their positions. The two smallest bridesmaids walked in front of the bride scattering rose petals as they went. The two other bridesmaids once again held Princess Bonnie's train followed by Samuel and Harry. Clara followed scattering more rose petals.

The guests rose to their feet as the Admiral and Bonnie started down the aisle. Mary was stood at the aisle end of her row as the bride on her father's arm came by. Now older and wiser, she caught Bonnie's eye as she passed her, she smiled and bowed her head knowing she was in the company of true royalty. Bonnie smiled back at her, her regal yet forgiving smile said it all.

Princess Bonnie looked ahead as 'Lelland' stood aside and placed her hand in Bobo's.

It was said that the folk around had never seen such a splendid and majestic affair. People gathered and celebrated with music and dancing. Streamers of all colours hung from the houses. Pipes sounded. The crowds cheered. The bells peeled. It was a joyous occasion.

Admiral Yelland had long been busy making arrangements for the newly wed couple to return to their native home, and now the time had come for them to depart. His coach and driver would be at their disposal and they would make the trip to the coastal port of Baymouth over two days. The Clipper ship 'Pearlstar' would be waiting for them at Baymouth Harbour and it's Captain was Mr. Hamley. The 'Pearlstar' had been in dock for the past two weeks, taking on cargo and supplies and making any necessary repairs ready for it's long voyage across the ocean.

It was a heart-rending time for Bonnie, all along she had wanted to go back to her homeland, but she had been with 'Lelland' for the major part of her young life and it troubled her to think that she may never see him again, but now she had Bobo, and she knew that he would make things wonderful.

The coach was packed with everything ready. With tears in her eyes Bonnie and Bobo waved farewell to the watching crowd lining the driveway. Admiral Yelland with his wife Harriet and Clara and even Mary, stood on the steps to see them off. The coach driver flicked his whip and with a 'giddee-up' the couple began their journey home. The Admiral had arranged with the driver of the carriage to make two very special stops on their way.

As evening drew in on the first night the coach lumbered into the large courtyard of *The Wild Boar*. Bonnie, was very young when she saw this place for the first time, but she recognised it immediately and smiled with pleasure. Nothing much had changed over the years. The large sign was still swinging in the wind but the boar was now freshly painted. The portly Landlord with his wife stood in the doorway with the light from within throwing their long shadows out to greet them.

Bonnie and Bobo made their way over and were welcomed by the waiting couple. They were a little older now, Bonnie thought, but she still recognized their faces.

They had some food ready for the travellers, and after reminiscing about the curly headed little girl, they were shown to the room where Bonnie had stayed all that time ago. Everything in the room was different, but she went straight to the window, and could see the driver of the carriage tending the horses. Bonnie thanked the Landlady who had little tears in the corner of her eyes.

Morning came quickly, and after something to eat and a tearful goodbye, the couple were once again travelling on towards the sea.

They journeyed on many miles getting ever closer to the seaport of Baymouth where the ship would be anchored waiting to take them *'home'*.   There was one other important stop to make, and the driver of the carriage pulled on the reins and the horses clip-clopped into the cobbled courtyard of the black and white inn called *The 'Lion'* . Bonnie turned to Bobo and held her hands up and made a roaring sound. Bobo laughed.

"I remember this place very well," she said, "The painting of the lion reminded me so much of home when 'Lelland' first brought me here*."*

Bobo squeezed her hand, "I do love you." he said.

They made their way through the large oak door and sat at a table. The light in the room was dim but the flickering fire was welcoming. The innkeeper came over with food and Bonnie at once recognized his jolly smile and gruff voice, and he, was quick to see in her face, the little black girl from many years ago. They talked for a while and soon they were on their way again, and it was Bonnie now that had tears in her eyes. Bobo held her tight.

Soon they could smell the salty sea air and way in front of them around the bay they could see the large ship anchored off shore in the dark blue green sea. Their carriage came to a gentle stop in the narrow cobbled street, and the driver showed them the inn where they were to stay that night, as the high tide they would sail on would not occur until the next evening.

The driver unloaded the carriage at the inn and went to stable the horses. He made his farewell to the couple and wished them a good voyage. Bonnie and Bobo spent their time walking around the fishing port, before returning to the inn. They had such a lot of plans to make for their future.

The next morning dawned bright. The couple headed for the harbour wall and from there they watched the hustle and bustle of this busy fishing port for most of the day. Many carriages trundled back and forth along the cobbled coastal road, and one in particular they watched with startled interest as it travelled at great speed, coming to a clattering halt with the horses breathing heavily and stamping their feet. From this carriage alighted the distinguished Admiral Yelland who they recognized immediately. They both waved and made their way up towards him.

"You have come to see us off, how wonderful!" Exclaimed Bonnie. "I thought we would never see you again."

'Lelland' took her hand. "I did want to see you set sail," he said, "but that is not the only reason why I have followed you. There are two people here that I would like you to meet before you set sail." He led her up to the carriage on the coastal road. Bobo followed.

Bonnie could not think who would possibly want to meet her, but she did not question 'Lelland'.

'Lelland' helped her into the carriage and she sat facing two people. The carriage was a little gloomy after the bright sunlight and it took her a few seconds for her eyes to become accustomed to the shadows. 'Lelland' and Bobo stood outside. Suddenly she realised who these people were, but she could say nothing, she just sat there looking from one face to the other.

"Do you recognize us? Little Black Pearl….our Little Black Pearl, how we have missed you. We have thought about you every single day that we have been in this strange land."

"Fa….Father, is it really you? Mother……I have missed you both so much." She threw her arms around them and tears began to run down her face. "Bobo, see who is here."

Bobo was so overwhelmed at the sight of the King and Queen of his homeland, that he was speechless.

" 'Lelland…Lelland, you did this for me, I can never thank you enough." Bonnie spoke through her tears.

"It was Her Majesty's doing," he said "we had spoken about things, and she requested that her subjects throughout the country should look for your parents, and her endeavours were successful. She then arranged a carriage to be here before the 'Pearlstar' set sail. We were worried that the ship might sail before we arrived."

"Oh! Thank you 'Lelland'....thank you," and with that she hugged him. "I shall miss you." She whispered.

"We are sailing on the evening tide," Bobo said, "see, there is a row boat coming ashore now."

"Captain Hamley will be with you on this voyage, and he has a great surprise for you." Admiral Yelland said. He smiled, and would say no more.

Admiral Yelland spoke to the sailors as they came ashore from the rowing boat, and he directed them to collect the small amount of luggage from the carriage and from the inn, and once again with mixed emotions, tears and smiles, they waved goodbye to the Admiral. Bonnie and Bobo, with the King and Queen, were rowed out to the waiting Clipper ship 'Pearlstar'.

The sea was very calm as the sailors rowed to the waiting ship, and as they came along side Bonnie saw the very friendly face of the Captain looking over the rail of the vessel.

"Joe, oh! Joe, I have thought of you often." Bonnie exclaimed. *"You are not the cabin boy now."* She gave a little giggle. "Am I to call you *'Sir'* now, or is it *'Captain Hamley'?"*

"Bonnie, it's lovely to see you look so well and happy." Joe replied as they embraced.

"This is my father and mother, who are now freed slaves, and this is Bobo my new husband, who has travelled many miles looking for me since we were separated as children." She breathed excitedly. "I am so happy!"

Joe smiled and shook hands with the new passengers.

"Bonnie, look who has also come to greet you, we moved together when I changed ships."

"It's Alfie, hello Alfie." Bonnie stooped down and picked up the ship's cat, she held him gently and stroked his silky fur, and the cat purred loudly. "I think he remembers me."

At Joe's signal the boson gave a loud shout. "Weigh anchor." And sailors began to work, they unfurled the sails and the ship was under way. Everyone waved vigorously to the Admiral who was still in sight standing on the waters edge and Bonnie waved until she could see him no more.

The glorious glowing orange sun began to set in a perfect cloudless sky.

Bonnie knew that this day was going to be the beginning of a wonderful new life.

THE END

Lightning Source UK Ltd.
Milton Keynes UK
UKHW02f1152170518
322697UK00005B/44/P